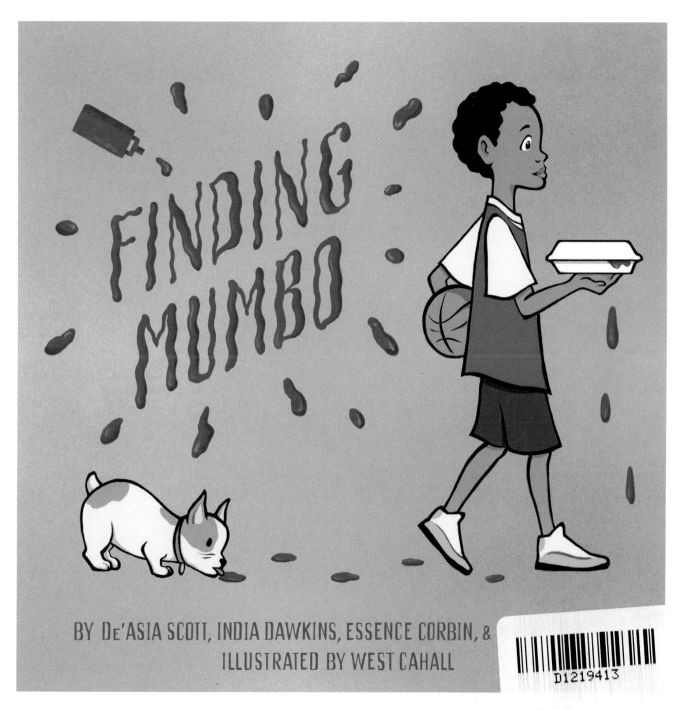

FINDING MUMBO

BY De'ASIA SCOTT, INDIA DAWKINS, ESSENCE CORBIN, &
ILLUSTRATED BY WEST CAHALL

Reach Incorporated | Washington, DC

Shout Mouse Press

Reach Education, Inc. / Shout Mouse Press
Published by
Shout Mouse Press, Inc.

Shout Mouse Press is a nonprofit writing and publishing program dedicated to amplifying unheard voices. This book was produced through Shout Mouse writing workshops and in collaboration with Shout Mouse artists and editors.

Shout Mouse Press empowers writers from marginalized communities to tell their own stories in their own voices and, as published authors, to act as agents of change. In partnership with other nonprofit organizations serving communities in need, we are building a catalog of inclusive, mission-driven books that engage reluctant readers as well as open hearts and minds.

Learn more and see our full catalog at www.shoutmousepress.org.

This book is dedicated
to everyone who loses focus
every once in a while.
Stay focused...

OR YOU MIGHT
LOSE YOUR DOG!

Rahim and Mumbo had always been best friends.

They played basketball together,

watched scary movies together,

and ate chicken and mumbo sauce together, too.

Rahim loved Mumbo, but lately he did NOT love the chores that came with him. In fact, he did not love any chores any more.

All he loved was basketball.

His Dad was always telling him
to be more responsible.
"Get up on time."
"Clean your room."
"Walk Mumbo."
"Take out the trash."
"Do your homework."

Rahim just rolled his eyes.

On the last day of practice before the big game, Rahim was running late. He had to hurry. If he was late again, Coach said he couldn't start. So Rahim grabbed his bag and his ball and his Jordan 13s and headed towards the door.

Mumbo pawed at the door and jumped on Rahim's leg.

"Sorry Mumbo, I don't have time."

"I don't think so," his dad said. "Son, if you don't take that dog out, you will not be playing tomorrow."

"Ugh!" said Rahim. He grabbed Mumbo's leash and slammed the door.

They walked down the block to Jefferson Street.

They walked by Ms. Johnson on her porch, Tyrone on his bike, and lil' baby J and Johnny play-fighting across the street.

Mumbo barked at all of them.

Rahim yelled, "Dang Mumbo, you always in the way. I'm gonna be late!"

Mumbo's tail drooped.

"Look, I know I haven't been that fun lately, but I got a big game coming up. You understand, right, man?"

Mumbo just looked at him confused.

Soon they reached Barry Farms Rec Center. They went inside but the lady at the desk stopped them. She pulled down her glasses.

"Unh uh, what are you doing? You know you can't bring him in here. Go tie him up outside. He'll be a'ight."

Rahim tied Mumbo up and ran to practice.

Rahim's friends, Fat Mike and Marcus, were already there, running laps.

Rahim joined them and fell into line.

He made it just in time.

That day, Rahim had a great practice.

He made three-pointers, crossed up Fat Mike, and got high-fived by Coach.

He knew he was going to start.

When practice was over, they did their last huddle. Coach told them to get some sleep and they all dapped each other up. Then Rahim, Marcus, and Fat Mike ran outside to get Mumbo.

"Ain't no dog out here," Marcus said.

Rahim turned to the lady at the desk. "I thought you said you had him. Where's my dog?"

"Little boy, I ain't no babysitter," she said.

Rahim saw little Tyrone chilling with his friends.

"Did you see what happened?"

"Uh, yeah. You tied him to somebody's bike, and they got mad and untied him," he said.

All the kids started laughing.

"My dad is gonna kill me," said Rahim. "We have to get him back."

"How we gonna get him back?" asked Marcus.

"We gotta go to the Carry Out," said Rahim.

"Yeah, I'm hungry," said Fat Mike.

"No, fool, so we can get some mumbo sauce for my man Mumbo! You know he loves that stuff even more than chewing shoes."

"Ain't that the truth," said Fat Mike.

On the way to the Carry Out, they walked by Ms. Johnson again.

"Hey baby! Where y'all going looking all musty?"

"Carry Out," Marcus said.

"We're looking for Mumbo. Have you seen him?" Rahim asked.

"No, but why you going to King City? Mumbo don't want that nasty sweet orange sauce."

"So what type of sauce does Mumbo like?" Fat Mike asked.

Ms. Johnson smiled.

"Back in my day we used to say,

If it Ain't RED it's DEAD

So they decided not to go to King City. Instead, they headed for Good Hope.

Rahim and his friends walked up to the counter.

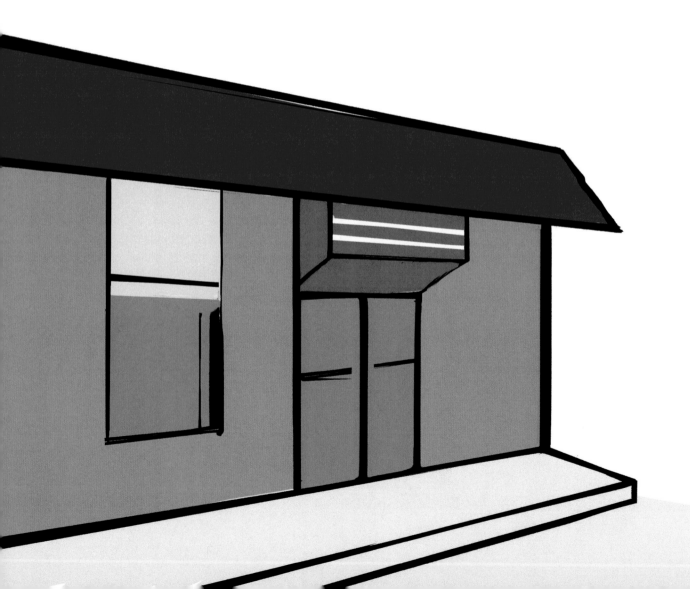

"Hey, what's up?" the man asked.
"Where's that crazy dog?"
"I'm looking for him. Have you seen him?"
"No, but I know he loves our sauce. You should take some to help track him down."

Rahim's eyes started to water. He was getting worried. If he didn't find Mumbo, his dad wouldn't let him play basketball!

Mumbo had one more favorite Carry Out.

It was starting to get dark, so they had to hurry. But Rahim walked slowly with his head down.

He was losing hope.

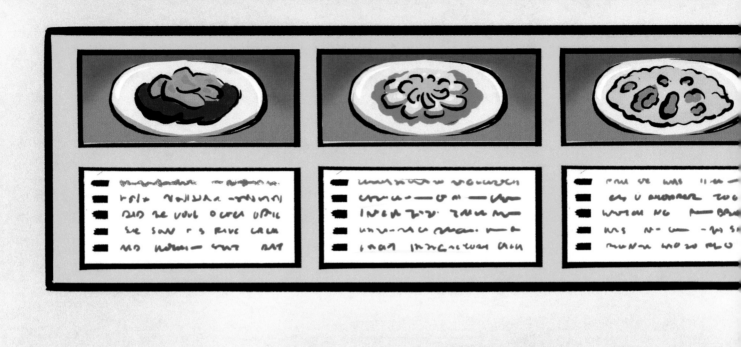

"Why the sad face?" the woman at Sunny's Carry Out asked.

"Have you seen Mumbo?" asked Rahim.

"I'm sorry, he hasn't been here," she said.

Fat Mike stepped up and interrupted.

"Well, can I get four wings with extra mumbo sauce on the side?"

"Come on, man!" said Rahim.

"What?" said Fat Mike.

By this time the sun was down, and Mumbo still had not shown up. Rahim wondered if he would ever see Mumbo again.

"I don't even care about basketball anymore. I just want my dog back."

"Man, you should've been taking care of business," said Marcus. "You gotta focus. I mean, you tied Mumbo to a bike!"

"I wasn't paying attention," said Rahim.

"EXACTLY!" said Marcus.

"Yeah," Fat Mike agreed with chicken in his mouth. "Basketball ain't life."

"I hear you," said Rahim.

The streetlights came on, so it was time to go home.

"Good luck man," Fat Mike said. "I hope you find Mumbo."

They dapped each other up and parted ways.

Rahim walked home with his head down, thinking that he had lost his best friend forever.

When Rahim got home, his dad was outside waiting. Rahim walked up sluggish and hunched over. He dropped his gym bag on the porch.

"Dad, I'm sorry, I didn't mean it."

"What are you talking about?" his dad asked.

"I lost Mumbo, my grades are terrible, my room's a mess, and did I mention I lost Mumbo? I messed up and now Mumbo's really gone."

Rahim sat down, put his head in his hands, and started to cry.

Suddenly, Mumbo ran up and licked the mumbo sauce off Rahim's hand. Rahim's dad started laughing.

Rahim's eyes got big and his tears became tears of joy.

"Mumbo!" he yelled.

"Are you going to tell me what happened?" his Dad asked.

"Nope," Rahim said. "But trust me. From now on, I got this."

About the Authors

DE'ASIA SCOTT

is a 15-year-old junior at Dunbar High School. She is a cheerleader who is also a Rales Leadership Council member with Reach. This is her second published children's book with Reach and Shout Mouse. She is also the author of *Speak! Amaya Finds Her Voice* (2017). She wrote this book because she knows what not paying attention gets you.

INDIA DAWKINS

is a 17-year-old senior at Anacostia High School. She's a happy person. This is her first book. She wanted to write this story because growing up she loved reading, and she loves imagining kids having fun reading her book.

ESSENCE CORBIN

is a 17-year-old junior at Washington Leadership Academy. She likes clothes and everything about clothes, money and everything about money, food and everything about food, and getting her hair done. She wrote this book to share her experience about what it's like growing up in D.C... and about how much she loves mumbo sauce.

MALIK SMITH

is a 17-year-old senior at Dunbar High School. He likes to explore and go to new places. This is his first children's book with Reach and Shout Mouse. He hopes by reading and enjoying this story his readers will learn the importance of responsibility.

BARRETT SMITH served as Story Coach for this book.
HAYES DAVIS served as Head Story Coach for this year's series.

About the Illustrator

WEST CAHALL
is an illustrator and designer from Washington, D.C. She loves animation, branding, comics, and research-based, informational design. She admires Reach and Shout Mouse's missions and hopes to honor their values of inclusion and accessibility, especially as they relate to the art world, narrative media, and her city. You can see her work at westcahall.com.

Writers and artists at work

Acknowledgments

For the sixth summer in a row, teens from Reach Incorporated were issued a challenge: compose original children's books that will both educate and entertain young readers. Specifically, these teens were asked to create inclusive stories that reflect the realities of their communities, so that every child has the opportunity to relate to characters on the page. And for the sixth summer in a row, these teens have demonstrated that they know their audience, they believe in their mission, and they take pride in the impact they can make on young lives.

Thirteen writers spent the month of July brainstorming ideas, generating potential plots, writing, revising, and providing critiques. Authoring quality books is challenging work, and these authors have our immense gratitude and respect: Talik, Synia, Jada, Temil, Trevon, Kahliya, De'Asia, India, Essence, Malik, Brittany, Dartavius, and Don'nayah.

These books represent a collaboration between Reach Incorporated and Shout Mouse Press, and we are grateful for the leadership provided by members of both teams. From Reach, John Gass contributed meaningfully to discussions and morale, and the Reach summer program leadership of Luisa Furstenberg-Beckman kept us organized and well-equipped. From the Shout Mouse Press team, we thank Head Story Coach Hayes Davis, who oversaw this year's workshops, and Story Coaches Holly Bass, Sarai Johnson, Barrett Smith, and Eva Shapiro for bringing both fun and insight to the project. We can't thank enough illustrators Jiaqi Zhou, Liu Light, West Cahall, and India Valle for bringing these stories to life with their beautiful artwork. Finally, Amber Colleran brought a keen eye and important mentorship to the project as the series Art Director and book designer. We are grateful for the time and talents of these writers and artists!

Finally, we thank those of you who have purchased books and cheered on our authors. It is your support that makes it possible for these teen authors to engage and inspire young readers. We hope you smile as much while you read as these teens did while they wrote.

Mark Hecker,
Reach Incorporated

Kathy Crutcher,
Shout Mouse Press

About Reach Incorporated

Reach Incorporated develops grade-level readers and capable leaders by preparing teens to serve as tutors and role models for younger students, resulting in improved literacy outcomes for both.

Founded in 2009, Reach recruits high school students to be elementary school reading tutors. Elementary school students average 1.5 grade levels of reading growth per year of participation. This growth – equal to that created by highly effective teachers – is created by high school students who average more than two grade levels of growth per year of program participation.

As skilled reading tutors, our teens noticed that the books they read with their students did not reflect their reality. As always, we felt the best way we could address this issue was to let our teen tutors author new books themselves. Through our collaboration with Shout Mouse Press, these teens create engaging stories with diverse characters that invite young readers to explore the world through words. By purchasing our books, you support student-led, community-driven efforts to improve educational outcomes in the District of Columbia.

Learn more at reachincorporated.org.

Made in the USA
Monee, IL
25 August 2020